To a girl I've liked for a long, long time.
—B.R.
To JDL, who I always LIKE.
—M.L.

Text copyright © 2020 by Bob Raczka
Illustrations copyright © 2020 by Merrilee Liddiard

Book design by Melissa Nelson Greenberg

Library of Congress Cataloging-in-Publication Data available.
ISBN: 978-1-944903-88-6

Printed in China.

10 9 8 7 6 5 4 3 2 1

Cameron Kids is an imprint of Cameron + Company

Cameron + Company
Petaluma, California
www.cameronbooks.com

LIKE
BEST FRIENDS

words by BOB RACZKA

illustrations by MERRILEE LIDDIARD

cameron kids

Summer dragged

    like a book that started out good, then wasn't.

The boy was bored
like a frog waiting for a fly to buzz by.

So he climbed on his bike
        like a cowboy mounting his horse,
        looking for a new horizon.

He pedaled slowly toward the playground
like a policeman patrolling the neighborhood.

The playground looked like a junkyard—
grass overgrown, tilting slide, rusty swings.

A girl sat on one of the swings, twisting it into knots and spinning like the propeller on a toy plane.

To the boy, this looked like fun.

But like most boys his age, he was shy around girls.

Suddenly the girl froze

like a doe who knows she is being watched.

Then, like a ballerina, she stretched out her leg
and tapped an empty swing with her toe.

Like a pop can in the wind,
the boy rolled forward.

He got off his bike and let it drop
        like he'd seen the older boys do.

Hands in his pockets, the boy walked up to the empty swing and kicked it
like maybe he had something better to do.

Then he sat down and twisted the chain once
like he'd seen the girl do.

The girl twisted twice

like a teacher encouraging a student.

When both were twisted up tight, they let go and spun together
like two maple seeds freed from a tree.

Then they giggled
like best friends.

When the giggling stopped, the girl stood on her swing and balanced
like a trapeze artist.

The boy did the same
like her partner in a circus act.

Together, they swayed and smiled
like characters in a book with a happy ending.

31901066169527